FAIRYTALE NINJAS

The Glass Slipper Academy

PAULA HARRISON

Illustrated by Mónica de Rivas

HarperCollins *Children's Books*

First published in the United Kingdom by
HarperCollins *Children's Books* in 2023
HarperCollins *Children's Books* is a division of HarperCollins*Publishers* Ltd
1 London Bridge Street
London SE1 9GF

www.harpercollins.co.uk

HarperCollins*Publishers*
Macken House, 39/40 Mayor Street Upper
Dublin 1, D01 C9W8, Ireland

1

ISBN 978–0–00–858294–4

Paula Harrison and Mónica de Rivas assert the moral right to be
identified as the author and illustrator of the work respectively.

A CIP catalogue record for this title is available from the British Library.

Typeset in Century Schoolbook
Printed and bound in the UK using 100% renewable electricity
at CPI Group (UK) Ltd

This book is produced from independently certified FSC™ paper
to ensure responsible forest management.

For more information visit: www.harpercollins.co.uk/green

For Michelle, who saw the world inside this story

WAYBEYOND

SNOWFELL PEAKS

RIPPLING RIVER

HOLLOW MOUNTAIN

SHIMMERING LAKE

WATERBURY

MURKWEED LAKE

DIAMOND PALACE

SCORCH ISLAND

CHAPTER ONE

'Quick, Tufty! Hide in here!' Red Riding whispered to the wolf pup.

Grabbing a basket from the shop counter, she bundled him inside while her mum wasn't looking. Tufty burrowed down, squashing a batch of blueberry muffins. Then he poked his black nose back out again, gazing at Red with adoring brown eyes.

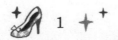 1

'This one's for Tom Thumb,' said her mum, pointing to another basket. 'Can you deliver it before your dance lesson? And don't forget your ballet shoes!'

Red pulled a checked cloth over the first basket to hide the wolf pup's fluffy ears. Then, grabbing her dance shoes, she rushed to the door. 'I'd better go! Snow and Goldie will be waiting.'

'Remember – don't go beyond the end of the lane,' her mum said anxiously. 'There are all kinds of dangerous things outside town – trolls, dragons, unicorns. The forest is full of them!'

Red rolled her eyes. She'd heard all this a million times before. 'Gotta go! Bye, Mum.' She dashed out of the door before Tufty could start barking and raced down the steps with a basket swinging on each arm.

Red delivered groceries from their shop –

 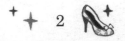

the Pickled Pantry – all over town, but she wasn't worried about meeting trolls or dragons or unicorns. Waybeyond was full of spells and magical creatures, but they never came into Hobbleton, which was probably the most boring place in the whole kingdom. Red had never, EVER met anything exciting, like firebirds or frost fairies. She thought she'd seen a dragon once – really far away – but it could have just been a very big bird!

Red delivered the basket to Tom Thumb, then took a short cut down a back lane and stopped by a row of signs at the very edge of town. Each sign pictured a magical creature with a big cross drawn over it. They read:

Fairies NOT Welcome

Unicorns PLOD OFF

Dragons KEEP OUT

Red gazed across the misty fields to Shadowmoon Forest and sighed deeply. She longed to leave town and go exploring! All kinds of amazing creatures probably lived in those woods. Why were the grown-ups so determined to keep every bit of magic and adventure out of Hobbleton?

The clock on the town hall struck half past nine. Red spun round, nearly crashing into a cart full of apples. She had to hurry up and find Goldie and Snow! Racing to the town square, she spotted Snow White coming out of the Silver Buttons dress shop where she lived with her family. Her pet squirrel, Blackberry, scampered after her.

Snow scattered some nuts for Blackberry and smiled at the bluebirds that had flown down to sing to her. Snow always had animals and birds following her around, wanting to be her friend. Red galloped up the street, and the bluebirds flew off in alarm.

'Hi, Red, you look happy,' said Snow.

Red grinned and lifted the checked cloth to show her friend the wolf pup in the basket. Tufty had fallen fast asleep on top of the blueberry muffins.

'This is Tufty! I rescued him from the bramble patch behind our house last Thursday, and I've been looking after him ever since. He's coming with us to the Glass Slipper Academy!'

'You can't bring a wolf to our ballet lesson!' cried Snow.

'Well, I can't just leave him at home by himself,' Red explained. 'Yesterday he ate my slippers and one of the armchair cushions.'

'Oh dear! I hope he doesn't get a tummy ache,' Snow said as she waved goodbye to her seven little brothers at the window.

On the other side of the square, a curly-haired girl came out of the Three Spoons Hotel. She kissed a little bear cub goodbye, before dashing down the street.

'Look, there's Goldie!' cried Red. 'Let's catch up with her.'

Snow and Red hurried past market stalls piled high with candles and grow-fast beans. Rushing past the bakery and the potion shop, they caught up with Goldie Locks at the corner.

'I hope we're not late!' said Goldie. 'Breakfast took ages because the guests kept wanting more porridge.' She brightened up. 'But at least Madame Hart's teaching us pirouettes today. I've been practising mine, and I think they're perfect!' She twirled round and round, until she fell over.

Snow tried pirouetting too. 'This is fun! Try it, Red.'

'No, thanks,' Red grumbled. 'I don't really like ballet.'

The three girls crossed the street and stopped in front of a majestic building with tall white

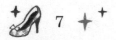

columns. A sign on the wall read *The Glass Slipper Academy* and girls and boys were rushing up and down the front steps, clutching their dance shoes.

Red, Snow and Goldie hurried under the archway and up the front path. Through the window of the main studio they could see a crowd of small children hopping up and down.

'The beginners' class hasn't finished yet,' said Goldie. 'Let's just wait here.'

She perched on the edge of the old wishing well in Madame Hart's rose garden. The well had once been the only magical thing in the whole of Hobbleton, but no one had got it to work for many years.

Sighing, Red set down her basket with the sleeping wolf pup inside. 'I don't want to do ballet today.'

'But what else is there to do?' asked Goldie.

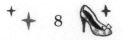

'I wish we could head off on a great adventure!' Red's eyes gleamed.

'Here you go then. Make your wish!' Snow held out a penny and nodded at the wishing well.

'There's no point!' Red burst out. 'This well is useless. It's the ONE magical thing in this whole town, and it doesn't even WORK!'

Her voice rose, waking Tufty. The little wolf pup poked his nose out of the basket and whined.

'Calm down, Red!' said Goldie, glancing in surprise at the wolf pup.

'I won't calm down!' Red growled. 'I'm bored of dance lessons, and I'm bored of this town. There's a whole kingdom full of fairies and dragons and trolls out there – except that we're not allowed to see any of it. When did YOU last see something exciting?'

Snow and Goldie exchanged looks.

 9

'Um . . . a couple of years ago – when Queen Arabella and Prince Inigo rode through town in their glass carriage,' said Goldie. 'They were on their way back to Diamond Palace. Don't they have fairies and unicorns there?'

'Maybe, but we've never actually seen any, have we?' said Red. 'And what about the trolls and giants and dragons? Where ARE they all?'

'Do you really want to meet a troll?' asked Snow.

'Yes! I want to see everything!' cried Red. 'I wish I could fight a troll, ride a dragon, chase a unicorn, wrestle a giant, fly with the fairies, explore Shadowmoon Forest and sail across Shimmering Lake!' And she grabbed Snow's penny and threw it into the wishing well.

The penny landed in the water with a dull plop. Then there was silence.

 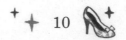

The door opened and a cluster of younger children rushed down the front steps.

'Looks like they've finished,' said Snow. 'Come on, let's go and put our ballet shoes on.'

Red trailed behind the others as they headed into the Glass Slipper Academy. Behind her the penny sank into the well, and ripples spread across the water.

A sudden gust of air whirled round the rose garden. There was a whooshing sound, and glittering light burst out of the old well. Cascades of silver, red, green and gold soared into the air, twinkling and turning until they faded into nothing.

But no one saw it.

CHAPTER TWO

R ed, Snow and Goldie hurried into the main dance studio where a piano stood in one corner and mirrors stretched along the walls. A sparkling crystal slipper was displayed on a huge pedestal high above their heads. The shoe had belonged to Cinderella, the first pupil at the academy, who now ran her own travelling dance troupe.

Red settled Tufty in his basket by the piano

just as Madame Hart glided in. The dance teacher leaned on her cane, her grey hair pulled back in a bun. 'Gretel and Aurora aren't well, so it's just you three today. Quickly now! Get your dance shoes on, and we'll practise pirouettes.'

Red groaned. 'Do we have to?'

Madame Hart gave her an icy look. 'Ballet teaches you agility and balance. You could learn a lot if you gave it some proper attention. Please put on your shoes while I fetch the piano music.' She marched out of the room.

'Now you've put her in a bad mood,' said Goldie.

'I was just saying what I think!' Red stomped up and down the dance studio, throwing her ballet shoes around in frustration.

One shoe soared into the air and landed on top of the pedestal where the crystal slipper stood.

'Oops!' said Red.

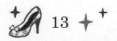

'Now look what you've done!' cried Goldie. 'You know Madame Hart doesn't like anyone touching the pedestal.'

'Don't worry, there must be a way to reach the shoe,' said Snow. 'Maybe there's something we can hook it with.'

The girls searched the room quickly, but there was nothing long enough to get the shoe down from the enormous plinth. Red tried climbing on a chair, but she still couldn't reach it.

'You could swing across from the curtain rail,' suggested Goldie, her eyes gleaming. 'We'll give you a leg-up.'

Footsteps sounded in the corridor. The girls froze, but the footsteps passed by.

'Do you really think that'll work?' asked Snow doubtfully.

'There's no time to try anything else. Quick!

 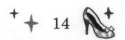

Join hands.' Goldie stood beneath the window, linking her fingers with Snow's.

Red placed one foot on their hands, and they boosted her into the air. Springing high, she grabbed the curtain rail and swung out, but she missed the pedestal and swung back to the window.

Pushing off from the windowpane, Red swung out again. This time she caught the edge of the pedestal with her fingertips and struggled for a foothold. Finding her balance, she lifted her ballet shoe from the top of the pedestal.

'Got it! Great teamwork.' She grinned down at the others.

'Hurry up and get down!' hissed Goldie. 'Madame Hart will be back any second.'

Red was about to jump off the pedestal when she spotted something shining beneath the crystal slipper – a small golden handle. Quickly, she lifted the slipper to get a better look.

'What are you doing?' asked Goldie.

'There's a little handle here,' Red called back. 'I want to know what it does.'

'You probably shouldn't touch it . . .' Snow said anxiously.

But Red couldn't stop herself. Reaching out, she pulled the gold handle.

A rumbling, juddering noise started up at once. Then part of the mirrored wall slid back to reveal a shadowy room. The girls stared at it,

open-mouthed. Springing down from the pedestal, Red crept towards the mysterious doorway and the three girls peered inside.

Racks of clothes and silver armour filled the small storeroom. Swords encrusted with jewels hung high on the walls, along with wooden bows and arrows. A crystal ball stood on a shelf beside some shiny candlesticks and a rolled-up parchment.

'Wow!' Red touched a silver shield with her fingertips. 'What's all this stuff doing here? These swords and shields are amazing!'

'Do you think they belong to Madame Hart?' asked Goldie.

'I guess so!' Snow looked round nervously. 'Maybe we should close the door before she comes back.'

'But these things can't belong to her – she only teaches ballet.' Red rummaged through the

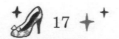 17

storeroom. 'This stuff is awesome! It's EXACTLY what we need to start our own adventure.'

'But we don't even know how to use any of it,' said Goldie, frowning.

'Then we'll find someone to teach us!' cried Red. 'Aren't you bored of cooking porridge and mending dresses? Let's take some swords and head into the forest right now. No troll can defeat us if we stick together!'

She tried to grab a diamond-studded sword, but it was fixed firmly to the wall, so she took a wooden training sword instead.

'I AM bored of porridge! Are you coming, Snow?' said Goldie, grabbing a second wooden sword.

Snow bit her lip. Then she picked up a bow and arrow. 'It sounds fun, but we'd have to keep it a secret from my little brothers. If they found out, they'd try to come with us.'

'Well, I won't tell anyone!' said Goldie.

'Me neither!' Red rummaged deeper in the back of the storeroom. 'Let's see what else is here.' She moved aside racks of clothes and boxes of arrows before finding a rolled-up carpet in the corner, tied tightly with rope. The carpet shook wildly as soon as she touched it.

Red dived on to the rug to hold it still. 'Something's trapped in here. Quick, untie the rope!'

The girls tossed their swords aside and struggled with the knotted rope. After a lot of tugging, Snow finally loosened it. Then suddenly the carpet unrolled, before shooting into the air, taking Red with it. The rug flew right up to the ceiling and hovered there.

'Whoa, what's happening?' Red peered down, gripping the edge of the rug.

'It must be
a flying carpet,'
Snow called back.
'Just hold on!'

The carpet shook out its
tassels. Then it lifted a corner and shot from one
end of the studio to the other. Turning a somersault,
it dived towards the ground. Red shrieked and
clutched the rug tightly.

Tufty gave a low growl. Leaping from his
basket, he chased the carpet all around the room,
barking madly.

'Oh dear!' said Snow.
'My dad says you should
never mess with
magical objects.'

'It's not my fault!' cried Red. 'I didn't know it was going to start flying.'

Just then, the studio door opened and Madame Hart swept in. Studying the scene with her sharp brown eyes, she rapped smartly on the floor with her cane. 'DOWN, carpet!' she snapped, and the rug drifted meekly to the floor.

Red climbed off, her legs wobbling. Tufty flung himself at the carpet, barking noisily. Then he caught the dance teacher's eye and hid behind Red with a soft whimper.

Madame Hart leaned on her cane and gazed at Red, Goldie and Snow. 'Well, well! You've found my secret storeroom. Maybe you ARE ready for something more than ballet moves after all!'

CHAPTER THREE

Red gripped her wooden sword tightly, her heart racing. 'Madame Hart, what are you saying? Is this stuff really yours?'

'Indeed it is!' said Madame Hart. 'A long time ago, I gave lessons in sword-fighting and other useful skills. Cinderella was my very first pupil and, when she was fully trained, we stored this equipment here secretly – ready to help the young heroes and heroines of the future.'

'If you helped Cinderella, then you can train us too!' cried Red. 'We want to go on adventures and see trolls and stuff, so sword-fighting would be really handy.'

The teacher shook her head. 'That would be very risky! Years ago, Queen Arabella issued a Royal Command saying that only her chief knight, Sir Scallion, was allowed to carry out combat training. Sir Scallion had told her that no one else could be trusted, you see, and that's when I hid all my equipment away.' She sighed deeply. 'But I can still teach you ballet . . .'

'Why would we bother with ballet when we could be learning something WAY more important?' cried Red.

Madame Hart tossed her cane aside and walked into the secret storeroom. Pressing the

catch on the wall, she released the diamond-studded sword. Then she swept the blade from side to side as she whirled round in a neat pirouette. The girls gasped and Tufty barked excitedly.

'Dance moves and sword-fighting are more alike than you think. Even pirouettes come in handy!' the teacher said with a smile. 'I'll show you what I mean. Take your positions, and I'll teach you some basic fighting moves.'

Goldie, Red and Snow moved into a space, and Madame Hart made sure everyone had a wooden training sword. Then she showed them how to swing their weapons and how to sidestep an attack. Goldie got the hang of it right away, and Snow was quick on her feet too, but Red swung too wildly, crashing right into the glass slipper pedestal!

Madame Hart beckoned them over to the storeroom and pointed to some ninja clothes. 'You should also learn how to move around unseen. These suits will magically change colour to match your surroundings. They won't give you complete invisibility, though, so you must practise ninja moves too.'

Goldie put one on and instantly blended in with the studio wall. With her body camouflaged, she could hardly be seen at all. Sneaking round the pedestal, she tapped Red on the shoulder, making her jump.

'But the most important thing I can teach you is to believe in yourselves,' said Madame Hart. 'It's easy to panic when things go wrong, but remember – you already have all the strength and imagination that you need! Promise me you won't forget that.'

The girls nodded and Tufty barked in agreement.

Red was about to ask a question about sword-fighting when she heard an odd rustling outside the window. She looked over to see a cluster of small brown creatures peering through the glass with beady black eyes.

Are they rats? Red wondered, and she stepped closer to get a better look, but the creatures scampered away into the bushes.

Madame Hart glanced at the clock. 'Goodness, where has the time gone? You'd better hurry home. Perhaps we'll do a few more sword-fighting moves tomorrow, but remember – not a word to anyone.'

'Thank you, Madame Hart!' the girls chorused as they dashed out of the door.

Red raced down the street to reach the Glass Slipper Academy every morning after that! Madame Hart wheeled in a small stepladder to reach the lever that opened the secret storeroom. Every day she added a new sword-fighting move or some ninja training to their dance lessons, and soon even Red could lunge and parry without tripping over her own feet. The three girls became faster and stronger, and Tufty got very good at chasing the flying carpet round and round the dance studio.

Three weeks later, the bluebells were just beginning to bloom in the hedgerows as the girls hurried down the road for another dance lesson. Tufty, who was wide awake for once, poked his furry head out of Red's basket to gaze at the strings of sausages hanging up in the butcher's shop.

'We should leave town right now and go off on

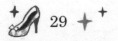

a real adventure,' said Red for the fiftieth time that week.

'But Madame Hart told us we're not ready,' Snow reminded her. 'She said we need to train for a lot longer.'

'We've done loads of practice already! I think we should just go,' said Red, taking a baguette from her basket and practising her sword-fighting moves on the nearest tree.

Goldie nudged her. 'Stop it, Red! Our training's supposed to be a secret. Remember – only the chief knight is allowed to teach sword-fighting by Royal Command of the queen.'

'That's a stupid rule!' Red grumbled, scratching Tufty's ears.

Turning the corner, the girls hurried up the steps of the Dance Academy and . . . straight into a troop of soldiers in the entrance hall.

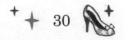

'What's going on?' gasped Red, staring round at all the guards.

A captain in a red uniform was towering over Madame Hart. 'I'm Captain Blunt from the Queen's Royal Guard,' he told her. 'We're here to look for Prince Inigo, who vanished from the palace yesterday. We've received information that you are responsible for his disappearance.'

'Prince Inigo?' said Madame Hart in surprise. 'I didn't even know he was missing.'

Captain Blunt looked as if he didn't believe her. 'Is that so? In which case, you won't mind us searching this place.'

Before Madame Hart could protest, the soldiers stomped through the academy, rifling through wardrobes and emptying boxes of tutus. The girls held their breath as the guards searched the main studio and sighed with relief when no

one discovered the secret storeroom behind the mirror.

'We can't find the prince,' a soldier told the captain at last. 'We've looked everywhere.'

Captain Blunt turned back to Madame Hart. 'Where is Prince Inigo?' he barked. 'He disappeared from his bedroom last night, and Sir Scallion says YOU are the only one with the cunning to get him out of Diamond Palace unseen.'

Red's eyes flashed. 'That's not fair! Madame Hart would never hurt anyone.'

'She's been teaching us ballet since we were three,' explained Snow.

'Shh, girls. That's enough!' said Madame Hart quickly. 'I can handle this. Sir, I can promise you that I did not kidnap the prince and I have absolutely no idea where he is.'

 32

'And I guess you don't know anything about the sword-fighting lessons you've been giving either?' the captain said nastily.

Red gasped. How did he know about that?

'Madame Hart, you are under arrest for the prince's kidnapping,' declared Captain Blunt. 'You will come with us immediately.'

Red, Goldie and Snow watched in horror as Madame Hart was marched out to the street and bundled into a waiting carriage.

'Poor Madame Hart!' cried Snow. 'Why would they think she kidnapped the prince?'

'It makes no sense! She'd never do a thing like that,' said Goldie.

'It isn't right!' Red snapped. 'And I'm going to stop them!'

She dashed back to the secret storeroom and grabbed a wooden sword. Then she rushed

 33

down the academy steps, waving it wildly. Tufty scampered after her, barking at the soldiers. But the men had set off at a gallop, taking the carriage with them.

Snow and Goldie pulled Red out of the way before she was trampled under the carriage wheels. The soldiers and Madame Hart disappeared in a cloud of dust, leaving the three girls staring after them.

CHAPTER FOUR

Red, Snow and Goldie watched the soldiers gallop away. A group of younger children, just arriving for their dance lesson, looked around in confusion. Tufty whimpered, so Red picked him up and hugged him.

'This is terrible!' gasped Snow. 'What are we going to do?'

'We have to go to Diamond Palace and tell

Queen Arabella that she's got it all wrong,' Red said firmly.

'You can't say that to the queen!' cried Goldie. 'Anyway, we don't even know how to get there.'

'Maybe there's a map we can use.' Red rushed back inside the academy, with Snow and Goldie following.

Searching the storeroom shelves, Red pulled out a large piece of parchment showing the whole Kingdom of Waybeyond. She gazed at all the magical places on the map and her heart began to race.

She pointed to Hobbleton – just a tiny dot in one corner. 'See – we're here. We can take a short cut through Shadowmoon Forest, cross the Rippling River and head straight for Diamond Palace. It won't take that long!'

Goldie folded her arms. 'Then what? We tell Queen Arabella she's got everything wrong and get thrown in a dungeon. Great plan!'

Red chewed her lip, thinking hard. 'We'll find the prince ourselves! That way we can prove it wasn't Madame Hart's fault he went missing. That soldier said he disappeared from his royal bedroom so we can start looking for clues there.'

Goldie looked doubtful, but Snow nodded slowly. 'We have to help Madame Hart,' she agreed. 'Think of all the things she's done for us. She's like a godmother to us all.'

'Okay, let's take what we need and go,' said Goldie, looking round the storeroom.

Red and Goldie grabbed wooden swords, while Snow took a bow and arrow. Then Goldie found three backpacks on a shelf, and the

37

girls stuffed some ninja clothes inside along with Red's blueberry muffins and a flask of water.

'I think we're ready!' beamed Red, giving Tufty a big squeeze. 'Don't worry, Tufty! I wouldn't go anywhere without you.'

The flying carpet rose from the floor with a soft swish and brushed against Red's leg.

'Do you want to come too?' Red asked.

Jiggling its tassels excitedly, the flying carpet did a somersault in the air.

'That's a very bad idea . . .' began Goldie.

'But it could really come in handy!' Red tried getting on to the rug, but it tipped her straight off again. Shrugging, she rolled up the carpet and stuffed it in her backpack.

Snow scribbled a note on a tiny piece of paper telling their families that they wouldn't be home

for tea. Then she opened a window and called to a pigeon. Tying the message to the bird's leg, she waved as it flew away again.

The girls crept out of the back door and headed for the edge of town. They stopped for a moment beside the signs banning fairies, dragons and unicorns from entering Hobbleton. Shadowmoon Forest lay straight ahead, its branches swaying in the wind. A puff of glitter rose from the treetops, as if something magical was hidden among the trees. Taking a deep breath, the girls stepped out into the wild.

'I've never left Hobbleton before. It's sort of exciting, isn't it?' said Goldie.

'We could meet anything out here!' Snow looked around, wide-eyed, as if a dragon might dive-bomb her any second.

The three friends headed for Shadowmoon

 39

Forest where a twisting, overgrown path led into the trees. A branch creaked, making them all jump. Tufty wriggled in Red's arms so she set him down and took out the map.

Snow peered into the woods with a shiver. 'I hope there aren't too many trolls and goblins in there.'

Red squinted at the place names on the map – Troll Cave, Goblin Hill, Grimstone Castle. She decided not to tell Snow. 'Let's try to get to Diamond Palace before sunset,' she said, rolling up the map and hurrying into the trees.

Tufty galloped ahead, barking joyfully as they set off down the twisty path. They passed shadowy forest pools and giant red toadstools that towered above their heads. Silver flowers covered the woodland floor, shining like a cluster of stars.

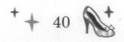 40

A strange tinkling noise started up, and Snow looked around nervously. 'Did you hear that?'

The tinkling grew louder, and tiny rainbow-winged creatures fluttered through the leaves. Darting here and there, they knotted a strand of Goldie's hair and knocked the map out of Red's hands. One hovered in front of Snow's face and showered her with glittery dust. Then they zoomed away again, giggling.

'Fairies!' breathed Snow. 'They're so pretty and sparkly.'

'They think they're pretty funny too,' Red grumbled, picking up the map.

The fairies reappeared a minute later, giggling even louder. The girls raced through a tunnel of trees and hid in some bushes.

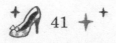

Peeking through the leaves, they sighed with relief when the fairies fluttered away into the sky. Scrambling out of their hiding place, they hurried onwards into a clearing with a crooked tree stump in the middle.

'Safe at last!' cried Red. 'We'll be out of this forest in no time.'

'Good! My legs are really tired,' said Goldie.

Red frowned at the map. 'I just need to find the path again. Now where is it?'

'We're lost, aren't we?' Goldie sighed. 'I knew we shouldn't have gone this way.'

The forest suddenly felt very quiet. Mist swirled through the trees like a soft white sea.

Snow nudged her friends. 'You see that crooked stump?' she whispered. 'Do you think it actually IS a tree stump?'

Red glanced at the odd stump with its

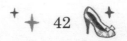

hunched-over shape and lumpy top. Was it the mist making everything look spooky or was that stump just like the trolls she'd seen in storybooks?

'We should hurry up,' she said quickly. 'It's this way.'

'Are you sure?' asked Goldie. 'Maybe you should let me read the map.'

'RAAAAHH!'

A slow rumbling growl rose out of the earth.

'What was that?' cried Snow.

The crooked tree stump quivered. Then it stretched out a pair of thick trunk-like arms.

'Uh-oh!' said Red. 'That's a troll!'

The tree troll yawned and stumbled to its feet.

'We should have put on our ninja suits,' Goldie whispered.

Red froze, hoping the troll would lumber away in the other direction. Then she glimpsed a fluffy grey shape sniffing around in the undergrowth right beside the troll's toes. Tufty was trying to dig his way into a rabbit hole.

'RAAAH!' roared the troll, reaching for the wolf pup.

'Tufty! RUN!' Red dropped the map and raced towards Tufty, clutching her wooden sword.

'RAAAH!'

The troll's gigantic feet hit the ground, cracking the earth open. Branches went flying as he grabbed at Tufty again.

Tufty shrank back, whimpering.

Red smacked the troll's leg with her wooden

sword, but it was like hitting a rock. The creature barely seemed to notice. Snow fired an arrow that hit the troll on the ear.

Goldie pirouetted past Red, grabbing Tufty first and then the map. 'Come ON, Red! I've got the pup. Now let's get out of here!'

Red dashed after her friends. The troll's eyes bulged as it thundered after them. Red glanced back. They'd never make it out of the woods in time! The troll was close behind – gaining on them with every giant step.

Suddenly she had the perfect idea. Leaping to one side, she let the troll get closer. Then, sticking out her sword, she tripped the creature up. The troll toppled over in slow motion, hitting the ground like a collapsing castle.

'Troll down!' Red jumped back, her heart pounding.

46

'We did it!' cried Goldie.

The three girls raced through the trees, and sunlight poured over them as they burst out of the thick forest. They stopped by a signpost to catch their breath. The sign read:

DIAMOND PALACE
2 Miles

Straight ahead lay a beautiful lake as clear as a mirror. Beyond that was a magnificent palace made from glass with glittering towers stretching into the bright blue sky.

'Diamond Palace!' whispered Red. 'And it's even more beautiful than I thought it would be!'

CHAPTER FIVE

Red, Snow and Goldie crossed a wooden
bridge that spanned the Rippling River.
Then they followed the path to Shimmering
Lake, where swans and river horses were
gliding through the water. A mermaid
played in the shallows, flicking
water drops into the air with
her tail. On

a rocky island in the centre of the lake stood a dark stone tower with one narrow window at the top. Red glanced up at the window, wondering whether anyone lived there.

Diamond Palace lay straight ahead with winged unicorns flying round its tall glass towers. They neighed to each other as they swooped through the air, their manes rippling in the wind. Snow, Goldie and Red hurried onwards, jumping across a narrow moat and climbing a golden fence to enter the royal gardens.

Beautiful fountains and glass statues were dotted among the vast flowerbeds. Soldiers stood at the palace entrance, and clusters of fairies swooped round the gardens. Red stared around, wondering how they could sneak inside the palace without being seen.

Goldie pulled the others behind a hedge as

two guards marched by. 'Get down!' she hissed. 'There are soldiers everywhere. We need our ninja suits.'

Crouching behind the hedge, they changed their clothes and stashed their weapons in their backpacks.

'Remember – stay super quiet!' said Red, tripping over her backpack and dropping her water bottle with a clang.

'Shh!' whispered Goldie. 'More soldiers! And who's that?'

The girls peered over the hedge. A knight in black armour was galloping up to the palace entrance. He took off his helmet and

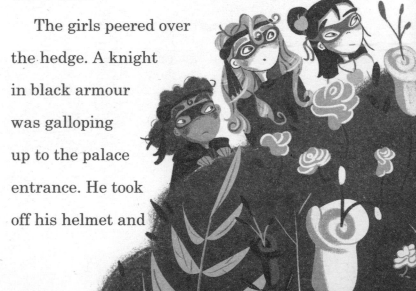

shook back his curly hair, admiring his reflection in the glass walls. A ring with a jet-black stone glittered on his finger.

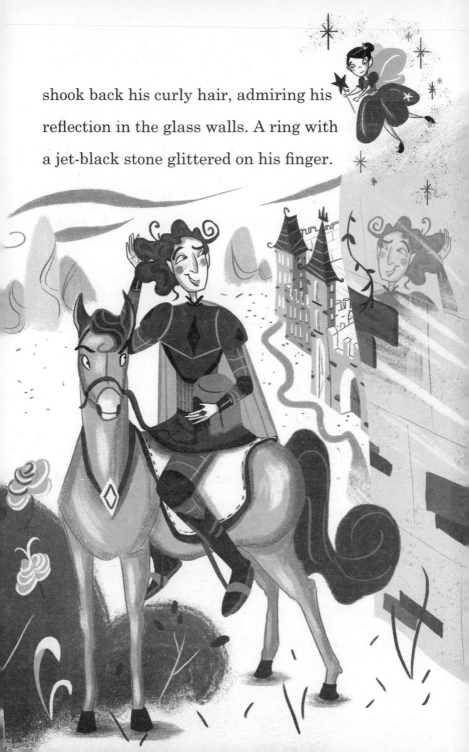

Climbing down from his horse, he got his foot stuck in the reins and tumbled to the ground. Turning red, he yelled at the palace servants for being too slow to open the door.

'Whoever he is – I don't think I like him very much,' said Snow.

'What a grump!' agreed Red.

'He's making so much fuss that we could easily sneak inside while no one's looking,' suggested Snow.

Goldie nodded. 'Then we can head for the prince's bedroom and look for clues.'

Red, Goldie and Snow crept round the hedge and ran across the gardens, hiding behind a fountain when the guards came past.

'How do we get inside?' hissed Goldie.

Red tugged on the vine growing up the palace walls. 'Let's climb up here and go through a

 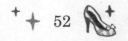

window,' she said, starting to scramble up.

'Are you sure it's safe?' Snow said doubtfully.

'Looks easy to me!' said Red, before losing her footing and sliding back down the glass wall.

She tried again, and Goldie and Snow clambered after her. They caught sight of Queen Arabella through the ballroom window as they climbed. She was sitting on her golden throne, clutching a toy train. Her head was bowed, and she was surrounded by fairies passing her tissues. The grumpy knight in black armour was standing at a nearby banquet table, loading his plate up with pie.

'The queen must be so upset about the prince going missing,' whispered Snow.

'Look, there's that knight in black again,' said Goldie. 'Do you think he's the one Madame Hart was talking about?'

'You mean Sir Scallion? I guess he might be,'

said Snow. 'But do you think—'

'DUCK!' Red shouted as a duck flew right past their heads.

Goldie glared at Red. 'We're trying to sneak in without anyone noticing.'

'Sorry – I forgot!' Red scrambled through an upstairs window and then pulled the others up after her.

As soon as they were safely inside, they tiptoed down the palace corridor, looking for the prince's bedroom.

'This must be it!' whispered Snow, pointing to a bedroom full of toys.

Boxes stuffed with teddies and toy dragons stood beside an enormous four-poster bed. Tufty, who had been snoozing in Red's backpack, woke up and whimpered, so Red lifted him out to sniff round the room.

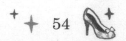

'That soldier said Prince Inigo vanished right here,' Snow reminded them, 'so there has to be a clue somewhere.'

Red checked behind the wardrobe and under the bed. Then she stared round the royal bedroom. Nothing looked out of place. 'I can't see any clues. Let's try downstairs.'

'Wait! There's something here,' Snow said quickly. 'Look – rat tracks. Lots and lots of them.'

A jumble of pawprints led across the window-sill as if a whole swarm of rats had been there. Tufty sniffed at the tracks suspiciously.

'What were they doing in here?' said Goldie.

'Stay back!' Red suddenly grabbed her arm. 'There's something under that rug and, if it gets any closer, I'll bash it.' She pointed her wooden sword at the lump moving around under the carpet.

'Is it a rat?' whispered Goldie. 'Or maybe

a fairy? Be careful not to hurt it!'

The lump gave an enormous belch.

Goldie frowned. 'It could be a fairy with tummy ache!'

Red dived forward. Grabbing the rug, she flung it aside to reveal a warty toad with slimy skin and big bulging eyes.

Goldie wrinkled her nose. 'It's just a frog. Ew, I think it needs a bath!'

'Urgh – what a smell!' agreed Red.

'I'm actually a toad not a frog,' said the toad.

Red stared at the creature in shock. Tufty yelped and ran under the bed.

'Actually, if we're being strictly accurate, I'm Duke Valazquez, the Earl of Waterbury,' the toad went on. 'And I can assure you I don't smell at all! I washed in fresh swamp ooze this morning.'

'You're definitely not a duke. Now shoo!' Red told him.

'Wait, Red! I've heard about spells that turn people into animals.' Snow crouched down beside the toad. 'Is that what happened to you? Did a witch cast a spell on you?'

'No, I brought the trouble on myself,' the toad said sadly. 'I was mean and jealous, and I refused to help my sister when she became the Queen of Waybeyond many years ago. I triggered an ancient curse that turned me into this!'

'Then you're the queen's brother – Prince Inigo's uncle?' said Goldie.

'That's right. Duke Valazquez at your service.' The toad bowed his warty head and gave a big smelly belch. 'Excuse me! Where are my manners?'

Red pointed her sword at the toad. 'Wait a minute! If you've been here the whole time, what do you know about the prince going missing?'

'I was outside in the gardens the night he disappeared, sleeping under a rock by a fountain,' the duke told them. 'But I heard the commotion the next morning and I saw the rat tracks on the windowsill. There's only one person who keeps an army of rats to carry out his orders.'

'Who?' asked Goldie, wide-eyed.

'Sir Scallion, the queen's chief knight,' said the duke. 'I'm certain he's the one that's kidnapped the prince, and now he's downstairs in the banquet hall, eating pie and pretending he's a good and honourable knight.'

'Are you talking about the knight in black armour?' asked Snow.

The duke nodded and gave another belch.

A memory suddenly sparked in Red's mind. 'And he has an army of rats! I saw rats at the window the day we discovered Madame Hart's secret storeroom. That must be how the soldiers knew that she'd been teaching us sword-fighting.'

'Sir Scallion uses his rats to spy for him,' agreed the duke. 'Unfortunately, the queen still believes that he's her most trustworthy knight, but I think he's hidden the prince at his castle in Shadowmoon Forest.'

Red frowned. 'What makes you so sure about that?'

'I heard Sir Scallion talking to his servant yesterday,' explained the duke. 'He said that he'd kidnapped the prince to get his old sword-fighting rival, Madame Hart, into trouble. It was his idea to lock her up in the tower in the

 59

middle of Shimmering Lake.'

'Poor Madame Hart!' gasped Snow.

Red gripped her sword tightly. Madame Hart was trapped in that tower in the middle of the lake – and all because of that knight in black armour. 'We'll find Prince Inigo,' she said firmly, 'and then we'll show the queen EXACTLY who's to blame!'

'Let me come with you!' said the duke earnestly. 'I really want to help.'

Thump,
THUMP!

Suddenly the bedroom doors were flung open. A troop of soldiers stood outside with their swords raised. The knight in black armour stood behind them, admiring himself in a hallway mirror.

'Sir Scallion! We've found those spies that

 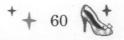

were climbing the walls,' said a guard. 'What shall we do with them?'

Red's heart pounded. How could they escape from so many soldiers? She scanned the room desperately. There was nowhere to go. They were trapped!

CHAPTER SIX

Sir Scallion stepped through the doorway, knocking a cluster of fairies out of his way. 'Get away, you pesky glitter bugs! There are too many magical creatures in this palace.'

Tripping over his sword, he fell to the floor. Red couldn't help giggling.

The knight glared at her as he scrambled up. 'I didn't expect these spies – or thieves – to be

so puny and pathetic. Three little girls! They're hardly worth bothering with.'

Tufty barked crossly, and Red grabbed him before he could get into trouble. 'We're not spies or thieves!' she told Sir Scallion. 'We're here to rescue the prince and I bet you know exactly where he is!'

Sir Scallion's eye started twitching as soon as Red mentioned Prince Inigo. 'What nonsense! Silly little girls meddling with things you don't understand. Guards, seize them! We'll lock them away in the tower along with that ridiculous dance teacher.'

'Madame Hart's not ridiculous!' cried Snow. 'She's an amazing teacher.'

The guards began to advance into the room.

'I'll hold them off,' Goldie said bravely. 'You two make a run for it.'

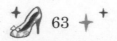

Red scowled. She didn't like being called a silly little girl. If Sir Scallion expected them to give up and hand themselves over to the guards, he was very wrong. She would show him EXACTLY what she could do. 'I've got a better idea,' she told the others. 'Let's climb back down the vine!'

With Tufty under one arm, she darted to the window. Swinging her legs over the edge, she felt around for a foothold. Snow and Goldie followed, and the three girls began to scramble back down the vine at high speed.

'Take me with you. Please!' croaked a voice. 'I really want to help.' Duke Valazquez, the warty toad, clung to the windowsill, staring down at them.

'Just jump!' cried Red. 'I'll catch you.'

The duke belched nervously as he crept closer to the edge. Then he closed his beady eyes and

jumped. Red leaned out to catch him before sticking him in her pocket.

'After them!' roared Sir Scallion, but the soldiers struggled to get over the windowsill in their heavy armour.

One guard tumbled out of the window and got tangled in the vine. Thrashing about wildly, he found himself hanging upside down by his foot until a swarm of fairies came to rescue him. Heaving him back over the windowsill, they bounced triumphantly up and down on his helmet.

'Stop hanging about!' Sir Scallion yelled at the luckless soldier. 'Get to the stairs, all of you! We'll arrest them in the gardens.'

There was a clanking sound as dozens of soldiers ran for the stairs.

Red jumped down from the wall and stared desperately round the palace gardens. Then

a great idea popped into her head. Pulling the flying carpet out of her backpack, she laid it on the ground.

'We're in terrible danger,' she told the rug. 'Fly us out of here right now!'

The carpet wriggled. Then it quivered. But, as soon as Red tried to climb on, it shot into the air and whizzed over to the fountains.

'That rug is useless,' said Goldie.

Snow glanced at the winged unicorns circling the palace towers, and her eyes lit up. 'We need to find the stables.'

'What for?' cried Red, but Snow was already running.

Together they rushed into a huge stone barn, waking up the snoozing unicorns inside. A row of carriages stood at the far end, made from silver, gold and sparkling crystal.

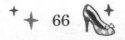

Taking out some muffins, Snow offered them to the unicorns. 'Quick – help me harness them to a carriage!' she told the others.

Red and Snow hitched two unicorns to the gold carriage. The animals shook their manes and stamped their feet, eager to get moving. Snow gave them another muffin each for luck.

Goldie flung open the big stable doors. 'Come ON, Snow! The soldiers have seen us. We've got to GO!'

Red bundled Tufty and the toad into the carriage. Then, leaping on to the box seat at the front, she grabbed the reins. Snow and Goldie jumped inside just as the unicorns bolted out of the stables, yanking the carriage after them.

The soldiers chased them, shouting. Some of them leaped on to other unicorns and galloped after the girls. Tired of being ignored, the flying carpet flew into the carriage and settled down on the floor.

Glancing back, Red saw Sir Scallion climbing

on to a black unicorn with huge wings. She gulped and shook the reins harder. 'Fly, unicorns! Up, up and away!'

The unicorns stretched their wings and rose into the sky, lifting the carriage with them. Soaring over the royal gardens, they circled round a palace tower before galloping away across Shimmering Lake.

'We've got to rescue the prince!' Red shouted to the toad. 'Where do you think Sir Scallion's keeping him?'

'Grimstone Castle – his fortress deep in Shadowmoon Forest,' croaked the duke.

'Faster! The soldiers are gaining on us,' yelled Goldie.

Red shook the reins again. Beating their wings, the unicorns climbed higher. Grey storm clouds blew in, and the wind rose, rocking the carriage

 69

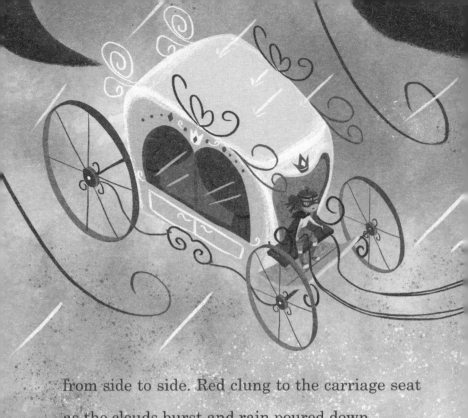

from side to side. Red clung to the carriage seat as the clouds burst and rain poured down.

Thunder boomed, and some cloud fairies whizzed past, lightning sparking all round them. The unicorns galloped faster, flying over Rippling River and onwards towards Shadowmoon Forest.

'The soldiers are gone,' called Snow. 'They turned back when the storm broke.'

Red twisted round to look, accidentally pulling one rein left and the other right. The unicorns got confused and flew in opposite directions. The carriage swung wildly, before starting to fall.

'Up, unicorns. Up, up and away!' cried Red.

Panicking, the unicorns dived towards the forest, pulling the carriage after them. The rain grew heavier, and the wind whooshed all round them. Red desperately yanked the reins again. More lightning darted past the carriage, and the unicorns whinnied in terror.

The carriage tumbled faster and faster. The treetops drew closer. Red held her breath. They were going to crash . . . and there was nothing she could do to stop it.

CHAPTER SEVEN

Red's heart thumped wildly as the unicorns plunged towards Shadowmoon Forest, pulling the carriage with them. The wind howled. Spiky branches stretched up towards them.

'We're coming in to land!' cried Red.

'You can't land on trees, Red!' yelled Goldie. 'It doesn't work.'

A second later, they hit the trees with a crunch.

The unicorns neighed in fright. Branches snapped beneath the heavy golden carriage, and it slid to the ground. Red scrambled down and released the unicorns from their harnesses. Shaking their manes, the creatures galloped away into the forest, unharmed. The thunder faded into the distance, leaving a steady pattering rain.

'Is everyone okay?' Red ran to the carriage door and yanked it open.

Goldie and Snow lay tangled up inside with Tufty and the toad.

'I'm fine!' groaned Goldie. 'I just landed on something lumpy.' She pulled her wooden sword out from underneath her.

Tufty leaped out of the carriage, barking excitedly. Red lifted the duke down. Then she noticed the flying carpet was twisted up in a

heap – shocked by the sudden landing.

'I don't know why we let you come along!' sighed Red as she rolled up the rug and stuffed it in her backpack again.

Snow beamed at a crowd of rabbits and bluebirds who had hopped over to help her down the carriage steps. 'At least we escaped from Sir Scallion. I hope the queen doesn't mind that we took her carriage.'

'She'll forgive us when we get the prince back, and that's exactly what we're going to do.' Red wiped the rain from her eyes and turned to the duke. 'Which way to Sir Scallion's castle?'

'Head into the darkest part of the forest where no sunlight can reach and no flowers can bloom,' the toad replied. 'That's where you'll find Grimstone Castle. That's if you can get there without Sir Scallion's army of rats seeing you.'

Snow knelt down to speak to the rabbits and the bluebirds. 'Can you help us find Grimstone Castle?'

The rabbits suddenly disappeared into their burrows and the birds flew away.

'I guess they don't like the place very much,' said Goldie.

'Well, I'm not afraid!' said Red bravely. 'All we have to do is find the prince and get him back to the palace. Sir Scallion doesn't scare me at all!'

An hour later, the rain was still falling. Red tripped over her millionth tree root and landed in a pool of mud. She scrambled up, wiping the dirt off. 'I'm never, EVER hiking through the deepest darkest bit of the forest again!'

'Too many brambles!' complained Snow,

pulling a thorny branch out of her hair.

'And the mud is even stickier than my porridge,' Goldie said gloomily.

'Courage, young friends! We must stay cheerful in these dark times,' said the duke, leap-frogging from one mud pool to the next.

Moving the carpet aside, Red rummaged in her backpack. 'We're running low on food and water,' she told the others. 'If we're stuck here at nightfall, we'll need to find something to eat.'

'Like what?' demanded Goldie. 'There's nothing here but mud.'

A little squirrel perching on Snow's shoulder scampered up a tree trunk. Shaking a branch, it dropped a cascade of nuts on to Goldie's head.

'Ow! Thank you,' said Goldie, rubbing her forehead.

The girls ate the nuts followed by some

 77

wild berries brought to them by a very friendly pigeon. Then they hurried into the trees before any more animals could bring them food they didn't really like. Pushing past spiky bushes and giant spiderwebs, they looked for the path to the castle.

'Why does Grimstone Castle have to be in the creepiest part of the forest?' groaned Goldie.

'Shh! Troll!' Snow pointed to a gigantic hairy foot lying across the path.

They had to clamber on to the troll's toes to get past. The creature gave a shuddering yawn just as Red reached the top of its big toenail. Stifling a yell, she leaped quickly from toe to toe. Then the girls ran, dragging Tufty and the duke with them.

After that, they wandered through a tangle of trees and, no matter how many times Red looked at the map, she couldn't work out where they

were. Darkness fell, and the forest came alive with hooting owls and rustling mice. The rain finally stopped, and a bright full moon peered down through the branches.

Stopping in a clearing, Red stared at the map again. 'The castle should be right here,' she muttered.

'You mean THAT castle with the big metal gate and spiky towers?' Snow pointed to the gloomy grey towers rising above the trees.

Red looked up. 'Oh, I didn't see that!'

Pushing their way through the bushes, Red, Goldie and Snow took their first proper look at Grimstone Castle. Moonlight poured over the high walls and metal gates, while stone gargoyles glared down from the battlements. Four grey towers jutted into the sky like giant's teeth. Tufty hid behind Snow's legs with a frightened whimper.

'Do you think Sir Scallion's there now?' whispered Snow.

'No, he's probably still at Diamond Palace,' said Red.

'Be careful!' croaked the duke. 'Even if Sir Scallion isn't there, the castle will still be guarded. He has a whole army of rats to do his bidding.'

'Who cares about a few little rats!' Red said airily. 'We've found the castle. Everything else will be easy.'

Goldie frowned. 'You REALLY shouldn't say things like that.'

'Why not?' demanded Red. 'Look what we've done! We've escaped from soldiers and trolls and really annoying fairies. We've done the tricky bit and now all we need to do is sneak into the castle and find the prince. Easy!'

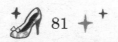

Goldie shook her head. She started to speak, but her words were drowned out by a ferocious roar. Loud wingbeats echoed through the trees. Red stared up in shock as a huge grey dragon zoomed out of the darkness and came flying straight at them.

CHAPTER EIGHT

RAHHH!

The dragon swooped through the sky, moonlight glinting on its scales. It struck the treetops with its wings, sending branches tumbling to the ground. The girls hid from view as the creature glided away into the darkness.

'Whoa!' Red gasped. 'So that's what a dragon really looks like.'

'Do you think it saw us?' asked Snow.

'No, looks like it's gone – at least for now.' Red crept out of the bushes and stared at the empty moonlit sky.

'Then let's find the prince before it comes back again,' said Snow. Goldie lifted Tufty into Red's rucksack, and Snow put the duke on her shoulder. Then they dashed to the castle wall and began to climb. Halfway up, a long thorny stem fastened round Red's arm. It tightened as

he tried to pull it off.

'What's happening?' she cried.

'It's got me too!' squeaked Goldie as a thorny stem wound round her ankle.

'The castle must have magical defences,' croaked the duke.

'Use your sword!' Red hacked at the magical thorns until they let go.

Climbing to the top of the wall, the girls jumped down into the courtyard below. Hiding behind some empty wooden boxes, they looked around for guards or – even worse – a large army of rats.

'Remember your ninja moves,' whispered Red. 'Keep to the shadows and don't make a sound!'

Waiting till the moon drifted behind a cloud, they sneaked across the dark courtyard. Red spotted an open window on the first floor. Finding footholds in the bricks, she clambered up and dropped inside with Goldie and Snow close behind her.

The girls crept along the narrow, lamp-lit corridor, careful not to make a sound. Pictures of Sir Scallion hung everywhere. Red opened a door and found the knight's bedroom stuffed with combs, mirrors and hairspray.

'There's no sign of the prince,' whispered Goldie. 'What if he's not here?'

'Sir Scallion must be hiding him somewhere,' croaked the duke. 'We have to keep looking.'

There was a sudden burst of laughter from downstairs. The girls followed the sound down the steps and along a winding corridor. They found themselves outside the castle kitchen, where a terrible burnt smell was drifting out of the door.

Red peered inside. A young boy and a pale woman with glasses were sitting at a table

playing a game of Dragon Snap. The boy wore a green velvet cloak and a gold crown. He won the game and gave a cheer.

The woman patted him on the shoulder. 'Well done, Prince Inigo. I'll just finish cooking the turnip soup. It smells good, doesn't it?'

'It's the prince!' breathed Snow. 'We've found him at last.'

As soon as the woman headed to the stove, the girls sneaked into the kitchen.

'Prince Inigo!' whispered Red. 'I'm Red, and this is Snow and Goldie. We're here to rescue you.'

'Rescue me from what?' asked the prince in surprise.

Red looked at the others for help. 'From Sir Scallion, of course! He's taken you prisoner.'

'No, he hasn't! He's brought me here so I can

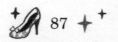

learn to be a Dragon Rider just like him,' said Prince Inigo. 'When I'm bigger, he's going to show me how to do it.'

'That's not true!' Red said urgently. 'Sir Scallion is a wicked knight and we need to get you out of here before that woman comes back.'

The prince shook his head. 'That's Mrs Muttle. She's playing Dragon Snap with me.'

Red's heart sank. How were they supposed to save a prince who didn't want to be rescued? She whispered to the others, 'What are we going to do?'

'Sir Scallion has been up to his tricks again,' the duke said sadly. 'He's convinced the poor boy that he's here to learn dragon riding.'

'You've got a frog that can talk!' cried the prince.

'Let me try something!' Snow said, kneeling down beside the little prince. 'I know you've had

 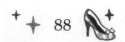

fun playing Dragon Snap, but, if you come back with us, we'll let you play with our wolf puppy.' She showed him Tufty, who was asleep in Red's rucksack.

The prince shook his head firmly.

'And we'll give you a blueberry muffin!' Red pulled out a very squashed muffin.

The prince shook his head again. The girls exchanged desperate looks.

'I know!' Goldie said quickly. 'We'll teach you how to pirouette like we do in our ballet lessons.' She spun round in a perfect pirouette and then gave a curtsy.

The prince beamed. 'I want to do that too!'

'We'll teach you as soon as we get back,' Snow promised, taking his hand.

Together they hurried away down the corridor. Footsteps sounded on the flagstones as they

reached a corner. Red peeped down the passage and her stomach lurched. Sir Scallion was here!

'Head for the front door!' she hissed to the others, before hanging back to listen.

Sir Scallion strode into the kitchen and checked his reflection in a silver serving dish. 'Where is that boy? You're supposed to be keeping an eye on him.'

'I don't know, sire,' Mrs Muttle replied. 'He was here just a minute ago.'

'Well, you'd better find him!' growled the knight. 'My brilliant plan doesn't work without him.'

'What plan is that, sire?' asked Mrs Muttle.

'Honestly, Muttle!' roared Sir Scallion. 'Is there cloth in your ugly ears? I've told you a million times. I'm going to be the one to find the prince and take him home again.'

'But he's not lost, sire. You made the rats

 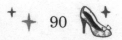

bring him here,' said Mrs Muttle, puzzled.

'I KNOW THAT!' snapped the knight. 'But the queen has no idea. And, once the prince is safely back at Diamond Palace, the queen will be so grateful that she'll hand the whole kingdom over to me. Then I shall put a stop to all this stupid sparkly magic. Unicorns and fairies will be banished forever, and children will be sent to the dungeon if they get in my way!'

A cold prickle ran down Red's back. Now she understood why Sir Scallion had kidnapped the prince. He planned to persuade the queen to let him rule the whole kingdom. She couldn't let that happen!

Running down the corridor, she caught up with the others. 'Sir Scallion's here and he's searching for the prince!' she whispered to Goldie and Snow. 'We have to hurry.'

Drawing back the bolts on the castle door, they ran out into the darkness. Halfway across the courtyard, the moon came out from behind a cloud and flooded the castle with silver light.

The gargoyles sat up at once. 'Burglars!' they squawked. 'Robbers! Thieves!'

Tufty woke up and barked, so Red lifted him out of her backpack.

'Who's sneaking round my castle?' Sir Scallion rushed to the front door and fell down the steps. He spotted the girls and angrily dusted off his armour.

'Not you three again!' he growled. 'Well, you won't escape this time.' And he pressed the jet-black jewel in the centre of his ring.

A faint scratching noise began. The

sound grew louder and louder, and dozens of rats poured out of cracks in the castle walls. Scuttling out of drains and holes, they rushed across the courtyard, their beady eyes fixed on Prince Inigo and the girls.

Goldie, Red and Snow raced for the castle gate, but it was chained shut.

'Up here, everyone!' Red began climbing the tall metal gate.

'What about the prince?' said Snow. 'He's too little to climb that high.'

Red hesitated. Snow was right. Prince Inigo was much too small to get over the gate.

Sir Scallion marched towards them with his rat army. Tufty barked crossly at the rats. The duke croaked in alarm and hid his warty face in Snow's shoulder.

'What shall we do? We're trapped!' cried Goldie.

'Maybe we weren't ready for an adventure after all,' said Snow.

'I want to go home!' Prince Inigo stuck his thumb in his mouth.

Red hugged him. 'It's all right – we'll get you home!' Her heart thumped as she faced Sir Scallion. She took a deep breath and tried to think of what Madame Hart had told them: *Remember – you already have all the strength and imagination that you need!*

This couldn't be the end of their adventure. There HAD to be another way out!

CHAPTER NINE

Sir Scallion stomped across the moonlit courtyard. 'Hand over the prince right now!' he yelled, 'or you're going to be in a LOT of trouble.'

He pressed the black jewel on his ring again, sending the rats rushing forward. Red quickly tossed them some blueberry muffins to keep them busy. She desperately tried to think. How were they going to escape? The way back inside

was blocked by Sir Scallion and the rats were closing in fast.

Suddenly Red noticed her backpack jiggling. Pulling it open, she frowned at the flying carpet inside. The rug shook its tassels, as if it wanted to tell her something.

'I don't have time to mess about,' cried Red. 'This is an emergency!'

The carpet ignored her. Shaking its tassels again, it shot into the air and did a little somersault to show how much it loved being free.

Red got a sudden idea. If only the carpet would finally let them ride! Then they'd be out of here in a heartbeat.

'Carpet?' she said urgently. 'We really, REALLY need your help. Please let us ride on you this time!'

The carpet wriggled as if it was thinking. Then it

whizzed out of reach. Red glanced worriedly at Sir Scallion. The carpet had never helped them before. Could she persuade it to help them this time?

Goldie rolled her eyes. 'Don't bother with that rug! It's just a waste of thread.'

Red tried again. 'Please, carpet! If you fly us out of here, you'll be a hero. Carpets from all over the kingdom will wish they were as brave as you!'

The carpet did another somersault, as if it really loved that idea. Gliding to the ground, it allowed Red to get on but, when Goldie tried to climb on too, the rug bounced her off again. Snow talked to it soothingly and at last the rug let everyone climb on.

'Are we going for a ride?' asked the prince.

Red swallowed. The rats were sneaking closer, their eyes glinting in the dark. 'Yes – a lovely ride,' she told the prince. 'Hold on tight!'

'How dare you!' roared Sir Scallion. 'You're not getting away that easily.' And he gave a loud whistle.

Wingbeats echoed over the treetops, and the grey dragon hurtled out of the darkness. Circling round the castle towers, it landed in the courtyard next to the wicked knight. Then it growled, showing off rows and rows of jagged teeth.

'Now we're really in trouble!' croaked the duke.

'Go, carpet!' yelled Red. 'Fly like the wind.'

The carpet rose into the air and whizzed over the tall castle gate. It shook its tassels rudely at Sir Scallion before soaring into the starry sky.

'Whee!' cried Prince Inigo, his eyes sparkling.

'To the palace – as fast as you can!' Red told the carpet.

The rug zoomed up and away, over the top of Shadowmoon Forest. In the distance, a golden

glow crept into one corner of the sky as dawn drew closer.

There was no room to move on the small carpet. Squashed together in the middle, the girls held tight to the prince. The wind whooshed round them as they went faster and faster.

Sir Scallion struck a heroic pose with his sword held high. Leaping on to the dragon's back, he wobbled and slid off again headfirst. Muttering angrily, he climbed back on and straightened his wonky helmet. The huge dragon rose into the air and sped after the magic carpet.

'Faster, faster!' urged Red. 'We have to beat them.'

The carpet shook its tassels crossly and slowed down. At once, the grey dragon edged closer.

'I think it hates being bossed around,' said Snow. 'You have to ask it nicely.'

Red sighed. 'I'm sorry, carpet! Please could you fly faster? I think you're the best flying carpet in the kingdom!'

The carpet did a little spin before speeding up again. The shadowy treetops flashed by below them. Then suddenly the forest was gone, and they were gliding over fields and meadows.

The morning sun rose over the distant hills and Shimmering Lake lay straight ahead, shining like a mirror.

A mass of flames burst from the dragon's mouth. Beating its wings, the creature drew closer and closer.

RAHHHH!

'Come on, carpet. You can do it!' shouted Red.

'We're almost there!' cried Goldie.

The gleaming towers of Diamond Palace jutted high into the morning sky. Red held her breath. They just had to get the prince safely back to Queen Arabella.

A dark shadow loomed over them. The grey dragon, ridden by Sir Scallion, swooped over their heads and zoomed in to block the way to the palace.

'Hello, dragon!' Prince Inigo waved at the enormous beast.

'I've caught you now!' bellowed Sir Scallion. 'Give up the prince or I will order Snafflejaw to attack.'

'We'll never give him up!' yelled Red. 'And we're not afraid of you.'

'You should be!' snapped Sir Scallion, taking off his helmet to smooth his hair. 'I'm the greatest knight in this kingdom. I was born to rule and no one will stop me, especially not three little girls like you!'

Prince Inigo stopped waving at the dragon

 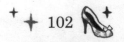

and blew a big raspberry at the knight.

The grey dragon lunged, snapping its jaws, but the magic carpet spun away and zigzagged across the sky. It circled round the tower in the middle of the lake.

Red spotted Madame Hart's astonished face at the window as they whizzed past. 'Don't worry, Madame Hart!' she called. 'We'll be back to save you . . .'

As they drew closer to the palace, a flock of unicorns rose into the air to meet them. A cluster of fairies whooshed into the sky too, and they all headed for the flying carpet.

'Out of my way, unicorns!' bellowed Sir Scallion, urging the dragon on.

Red felt the heat of the dragon's breath. The creature roared, and a flame from its mouth scorched the edge of the carpet.

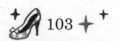

Diving towards the palace garden, the carpet plunged straight into a fountain. Everyone tumbled into the water with a splash. The carpet shook itself, cooling its burnt patch in the water.

'Splash-landing!' shouted Prince Inigo, flicking water into the air and giggling.

Red joined in and soon she, Goldie and Snow were madly splashing each other. Tufty jumped in and out of the fountain, while the duke swam around happily. Zooming back into the air, the carpet shook the water drops off its tassels.

The ground shook as the grey dragon landed behind them with a thundering roar.

'Now I have you!' Sir Scallion leaped down from the dragon's back.

He reached out to grab Prince Inigo, but lost his balance and fell into the fountain. Climbing

out, he emptied the water out of his helmet. 'My hair is ruined! And look at my lovely armour. You horrible girls! This is all your fault!'

Golden trumpets rang out, and Queen Arabella hurried into the gardens. She saw Prince Inigo and began to run, her satin train flowing out behind her. 'Inigo, there you are, my darling!'

Prince Inigo rushed into her arms and gave her an enormous hug. 'Mummy, I've been on an adventure!'

'Where did you go, my love?' the queen asked worriedly.

'Sir Scallion took me to his castle,' explained the prince. 'And these girls came to fetch me back again!' He pointed to Red, Snow and Goldie.

Red climbed out of the fountain, water dripping from her ninja suit. Tufty leaped after her, barking joyfully. Red walked up to the queen and managed a dripping-wet curtsy. 'Hello, Your Majesty! I'm Red Riding and these are my friends, Snow White and Goldie Locks.'

CHAPTER TEN

Queen Arabella looked at the girls in astonishment. 'My goodness! Where did you all come from?'

'We're from Hobbleton,' explained Goldie.

'And we learn ballet at Madame Hart's dance academy,' added Snow.

'We wanted to help the prince,' said Red, 'and to prove it wasn't Madame Hart's fault he went missing. We've fought trolls, climbed up castle

walls and escaped from an army of rats to get here!'

'Goodness! No wonder you look so dirty,' exclaimed the queen. 'Did you really do all of that? I'm not sure whether I believe you.'

The toad hopped forward. 'Your Majesty, these ordinary girls from Hobbleton are really quite remarkable and—' He broke off with a funny hiccup. His eyes bulged and his lumpy green body began to shimmer.

The queen peered down at him. 'Eric . . . is that you?'

A gust of wind swirled through the palace gardens, and suddenly the toad vanished and a man with a rough beard appeared in its place.

'Eric!' cried Queen Arabella. 'It *is* you! My dear brother – where have you been? I've missed you very much.'

'My curse is lifted!' cried the duke, gazing at

 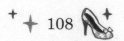

his hands and arms in delight.

'Maybe you had to do something unselfish to break the spell,' suggested Snow. 'So rescuing the prince finally did it.'

'I'm so happy to be myself again. Thank you, girls, for helping me.' The duke bowed to Red, Goldie and Snow.

The queen smiled at the girls. 'And thank you for rescuing my darling boy and for showing me who was really to blame for all of this.' She turned to Sir Scallion, who was still trying to shake the water out of his armour.

The knight squelched as he gave a bow. 'Your Majesty, I can explain . . .'

'Is that right? Because you blamed everything on poor Madame Hart.' The queen looked stern.

'These girls are lying about rescuing the prince,' said Sir Scallion, his eye twitching. 'They were the ones who took him away, and I simply tried to bring him back again.'

'But you said I was coming to your castle to learn dragon riding!' the prince piped up.

There was silence and Sir Scallion turned red.

'My dear sister, I believe Sir Scallion has been trying to take over your kingdom for a very long time,' said the duke.

The queen turned to the knight. 'Is this true?' she demanded.

Sir Scallion smoothed his soggy hair. 'It's obvious that I'd be a much better ruler than you! Your kingdom is overrun by unicorns and girls in flying carriages. This place needs order!'

'What nonsense!' Queen Arabella's eyes flashed with anger. 'Once upon a time, you were my chief

 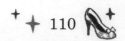

knight, but knights are supposed to protect others and YOU care about no one but yourself. You are banished from my palace forever. Leave this place AT ONCE!'

Sir Scallion glowered and tried to climb back on to his dragon, but Snafflejaw had started playing chase with Tufty. The dragon flicked his spiky tail and refused to let the knight get on. Cursing, Sir Scallion marched off towards Grimstone Castle, his armour still squelching.

'We must celebrate the prince's return!' the queen declared. 'You three girls shall be the guests of honour. We will have music and dancing and ice cream in fifty different flavours!'

But Red had already started running across the palace garden, her eyes fixed on the tower in the middle of the lake. 'Thanks, Queen Arabella! That's really nice of you,' she called back. 'But there's something really important we have to do first!'

CHAPTER ELEVEN

The flying carpet was still too damp to ride on, so Red, Goldie and Snow found some friendly unicorns to fly them to the island in the middle of the lake. Circling the tower on the unicorns' backs, they peered in through the dark window.

'Madame Hart, we're here to rescue you!' cried Red.

Madame Hart appeared at the window and

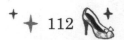

beamed at them, her eyes crinkling. 'Well done, girls! I see you've been having some adventures.'

Red desperately wanted to tell Madame Hart everything as they flew back to the palace together, but as soon as they landed the queen insisted that they come and join the party.

Everyone sat down to a magnificent banquet with a blackcurrant jelly in the shape of a palace and a chocolate cake with seventeen layers. There were cherry-blossom pies for the fairies and cucumber wraps for the unicorns.

After the feast, everyone walked down to Shimmering Lake. The merpeople played

their crystal harps, the river horses danced in
the water and the fairies sprinkled everyone
with rose petals. Red, Snow and Goldie watched

everything in amazement. Even Madame Hart, who was tired after her imprisonment in the tower, smiled when she heard the harps play.

Goldie taught Prince Inigo to pirouette, just as she'd promised, and suddenly everyone wanted to try it. The fairies were especially good at pirouetting but when Snafflejaw joined in, he accidentally knocked them into the lake with his enormous tail!

Red ate five pieces of chocolate cake before realising that she had a very strange feeling in her stomach. 'I think I miss Hobbleton,' she said in surprise.

'Me too!' said Snow.

'Diamond Palace is fun, but it's not home,' agreed Goldie.

So Red, Goldie and Snow packed up their rucksacks and found Tufty, who was still playing with the dragon. Red rolled up the flying carpet who had fallen asleep in a flowerbed. Then they thanked the queen and said goodbye to Madame

Hart, who had decided to stay the night at the palace and return the following day.

'Maybe Madame Hart will give us some more training once she gets back to Hobbleton,' said Red as they headed into the forest. 'I really want to improve my sword-fighting skills. Then I can defeat every troll we meet.'

'And I'd like to get better at using my bow and arrow,' said Snow.

'I want to climb a castle wall faster than a flash of lightning!' said Goldie.

They reached the Glass Slipper Academy just as darkness fell and changed back into their usual clothes. The wishing well in the academy garden glimmered gently in the dark.

'Let's meet back here tomorrow,' said Goldie eagerly. 'And bring your swords, bows and ninja clothes.'

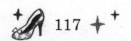 117

Snow nodded. 'And Tufty can come too!'

'First thing tomorrow,' agreed Red, grinning. 'There's a lot to do to get ready for our next adventure!'